S0-BFB-449

For Lauren – J.M.

For Bella – K.T.

Text copyright © 2004 Judi Moreillon. Art copyright © 2004 Kyra Teis.
All rights reserved. No part of this book may be reproduced or transmitted in any
form or by any means, electronic or mechanical, photocopying, recording, or by
any information storage and retrieval systems that are available now or in the
future, without permission in writing from the copyright holders and the publisher.

Published in the United States of America by Star Bright Books, Inc., New York.
The name Star Bright Books and the Star Bright Books logo are registered
trademarks of Star Bright Books, Inc. Please visit www.starbrightbooks.com.

ISBN 1-932065-49-0

Printed in China
9   8   7   6   5   4   3

Library of Congress Cataloging-in-Publication Data

Moreillon, Judi.
  Read to me / by Judi Moreillon ; illustrated by Kyra Teis.
    p. cm.
  Summary: Rhyming verses encourage parents to read and tell stories to
their children.
  ISBN 1-932065-49-0
  [1. Books and reading--Fiction. 2. Parent and child--Fiction. 3.
Stories in rhyme.] I. Teis, Kyra, ill. II. Title.
PZ8.3.M7975 Re 2004
[E]--dc22
                              2003020560

Read to Me

By
Judi Moreillon

Illustrated by
Kyra Teis

Star Bright Books
New York

Read to me
and watch me grow.
Tell me all
the tales you know.

For in this life,
I'll need a map.
Let it begin
upon your lap—

In picture books
  and nursery rhymes,
fairy tales
  from other times,

and every song
  your mother knew,

family stories,
  wise and true.

Read to me
every day.
Tell me stories
while we play.

In the bath
  and on the stair,
we can read
  'most anywhere.

Read the pictures
and read the lines,
words to nourish
hearts and minds—

books 'bout bikes
and teddy bears,
moons and stars
and broken chairs.

Read to me
    and plant the seed.
Make me want
    to learn to read.

Read to me
  and watch me grow.
Tell me all
  the tales you know.